W9-CAY-523

EAGLE VALLEY LIBRARY DISTRICT
1 06 0004346876

# The
# Show-Off

Moose and Hildy

# The Show-Off

by Stephanie Greene
illustrated by Joe Mathieu

Marshall Cavendish Children

Marshall Cavendish Corporation,
99 White Plains Road, Tarrytown, NY 10591
www.marshallcavendish.us/kids

Library of Congress Cataloging-in-Publication Data

Greene, Stephanie.
The show-off / by Stephanie Greene ; illustrated by Joe Mathieu. — 1st ed.
p. cm. — (Moose and Hildy)
"A Marshall Cavendish chapter book"—Copyright p.
Summary: Hildy looks forward to a visit from her cousin, Winston, but when he arrives he bores her and annoys all of her friends by declaring his superior intelligence and expertise on every subject, until Moose convinces him to try something different.

ISBN 978-0-7614-5374-1
[1. Egoism—Fiction. 2. Pigs—Fiction. 3. Moose—Fiction. 4. Friendship—Fiction. 5. Humorous stories.] I. Mathieu, Joseph, ill. II. Title.
PZ7.G8434
[E]—dc22
2007000253

The text of this book is set in Garamond.
The illustrations were created with Prismacolor pencil and Dr. Martin gray wash.

Editor: Margery Cuyler
Book design by Vera Soki

A Marshall Cavendish Chapter Book

Printed in China
First edition
1 3 5 6 4 2

mc Marshall Cavendish Children

*For Matthew and Shep, my show-off brothers*

—S.G.

*To my son Joe, with love and admiration*

—J.M.

# Contents

## Chapter One

# Here's Winston Now!

The front door of Hildy's house was open. Blankets hung from the upstairs windows. A vacuum cleaner roared inside the house.

"Knock, knock," Moose shouted. "Anybody home?"

The vacuum cleaner stopped. "I'm in here!" Hildy called.

Moose walked through the front hall to the living room.

"Careful," said Hildy. "I just waxed the floor. It's slippery."

"You can't be spring housecleaning," Moose said. "It's fall. Look."

He bent his head for Hildy to see the two small bumps on top.

His antlers.

They fell off every spring. And they grew back every fall.

At the first sign of the bumps, Moose and Hildy played a final game of checkers in front of Hildy's fireplace. Before long the antlers would grow too big for Moose to fit inside the house.

"Ready for our last game?" Moose asked.

Hildy was busily dusting the coffee table.

"I won't have time to play this year," she said. "I'm having a houseguest."

"You are?" said Moose. "Who?"

"My cousin Winston. He'll be here any minute."

"Great. Then the three of us can play."

"I'm afraid not, Moose," said Hildy. "Winston doesn't play checkers."

"Doesn't play checkers?" Moose said. "Why not?"

"Don't get upset," Hildy said carefully, "but Winston thinks checkers is babyish."

"Babyish?" Moose drew himself up to his full height. "Do I look like a baby to you, Hildy?"

"Of course you don't. But Winston's different." Hildy sounded proud. "He's gifted."

"What does that mean?" Moose grumbled.

"It means he has a high IQ."

"So?"

"So, he's really smart."

"At what?"

"I don't know. Lots of things, I guess."

"Smart about looking for food in the woods?" said Moose.

"Of course not, silly. He lives in the city."

"How about growing antlers? I suppose he has huge, magnificent antlers."

Hildy laughed. "He's not a moose. He's a pig, Moose."

"Then what's he so smart about?"

"I don't know. . . ."

Just then a horn sounded from outside. Hildy ran to the window.

"Why don't you ask him?" she said with a smile. "Here's Winston's taxi now."

Chapter Two

# An Expert on Everything

Moose and Hildy couldn't get a word in edgewise.

Winston started talking the minute they sat down to lunch. He didn't stop.

First, he talked about science. Then he talked about math. Now he was talking about computers.

He had been talking about computers for half an hour.

"My," Hildy said with a yawn. "You certainly are an expert on computers, Winston."

Winston chuckled. "You might say I'm an expert on almost everything."

"*You* certainly might," Moose agreed.

"After all, I could read by the time I was two," said Winston.

"You don't say?" said Moose.

"By kindergarten I was reading on a sixth-grade level."

"Is that right?"

"Pigs are very smart as a group," Winston said. "But, of course, I'm smarter than most."

"Of course," said Moose.

"Go on," Winston said. "Ask me anything."

"More cake?" Hildy said quickly.

"Too much sugar. And all that butter." Winston frowned. "Think of the calories."

"Yes, think of them." Moose smacked his lips. "I'd love another piece, Hildy. It's delicious."

"I watch what I eat very carefully, and I like to think it shows," Winston said. He patted his stomach proudly. "You might want to start doing the same thing, Hildy."

Hildy's mouth fell open.

Moose stood up. "On second thought," he said, "I think I'll go bird-watching."

"Good idea." Hildy stood up, too. "Come on, Winston. Moose is an expert when it comes to birds."

"I don't care for birds," said Winston. "They're noisy creatures. You stay here, Hildy. I haven't told you about electricity yet."

"Oh, goody." Hildy sank back into her

chair. "I can hardly wait."

"I'll be off then," said Moose. "Toodle-oo!"

"Be careful in the woods," Winston said. "It's full of wild animals."

"Are you being funny?" Moose said.

"I'm never funny," said Winston. "Why do you think I travel with this?" He held up a whistle that was hanging around his neck.

"What do you do with it?" asked Moose.

"I use it to scare off wild animals."

"Really? Does it work?"

Winston gave a sharp blast on his whistle.

Moose ran into the woods.

"My, my," Winston said. "What in the world got into him?"

Chapter Three

# An Expert on Flowers

Hildy called Moose the next morning.

"Winston and I are going on a picnic," she said. "I want you to come."

"Actually, it's such a beautiful day," Moose said, "I thought I might go to the dentist and have a few teeth pulled."

"Don't be funny," said Hildy.

"I'm never funny."

"Moose, please . . . ?"

Moose met them at the lake. They set up the picnic. Then Moose decided to go for a swim.

"How about it, Winston?" he said. "Care for a swim before lunch?"

"In that water?" Winston turned up his nose. "Not on your life."

"Why not?" said Moose.

"It's full of germs."

"What do you mean? I drink it and swim in it every day."

"Exactly," said Winston.

Hildy quickly stepped between them. "Why don't you and I go pick some flowers for the table, Winston?" she said.

"Allow me," said Winston. "I'm an expert on flowers."

"You might want to watch out for the—"

"Please." Winston cut off Moose with a laugh. "There's nothing I don't know about flowers."

Moose swam to the middle of the lake. He floated on his back. He blew waterspouts.

By the time he got back to shore, Winston was coming out of the woods.

"Look!" Winston called. He held up a large bouquet of flowers. "I found some clover, too. It'll bring us good luck!"

"Oh, Winston. How sweet." Hildy looked at Moose. "Isn't that sweet, Moose?"

"Like maple syrup," said Moose.

He peered at the shiny green leaves Winston had stuck between the flowers. "But I'm afraid that's not clover."

"I beg your pardon," said Winston. "I'm quite an expert on plants."

"Too bad you're not an expert on weeds," said Moose. "That's not clover. That's poison ivy."

## Chapter Four

# Itchy, Itchy, Itchy

"How's the patient?" Moose asked.

Hildy stepped outside and shut her front door quietly behind her. "Poor Winston. He itches all over," she said. "And I think he's embarrassed."

"He should be."

"Moose, be nice. Winston's my guest. I want him to have a good time."

"Why don't you rent a video camera so he can watch himself talk?" said Moose. "That would make him happy."

"It's not like you to be mean, Moose."

"Oh, all right," said Moose. "I guess it's not much fun being an expert on scratching.

What are you going to do?"

"I want to have a party to cheer him up."

"Who are you going to invite?"

"All of our friends, of course."

"You'd do that to them?" joked Moose.

"Moose . . . !"

"I'm sorry, Hildy. But a moose gets tired of being lectured to all the time," Moose said. "I may not be gifted, but I know a thing or two of my own."

"Of course you do. And you *are* gifted," Hildy said. "You're more gifted at being a friend than anyone I know."

"I am?" said Moose.

"Yes. Now, will you help me?"

"Aw, shucks. What do you want me to do?"

"Come help me decorate." Hildy opened the door and pulled him inside. "We'll blow up balloons, and bake a cake, and everything. It'll be fun, Moose. You'll see."

## Chapter Five

# Not a Party Animal

"All right," Winston called. "Everyone calm down!"

He was standing on a chair, facing the guests. "Since none of you is interested in reading out loud," he said, "we'll do math problems."

Groans sounded around the room.

"Winston?" Hildy tugged on his jacket. "May I speak with you for a minute?"

"Not now, Hildy." Winston looked around the crowd. "Okay. Let's start with something easy. What's twelve times twelve?"

Three guests at the back slipped out of the room.

"One hundred and forty-four!" Winston cried when no one answered. "How about ten times ten?"

"Are you sure he's Hildy's cousin?" Otis whispered to Francie.

"One hundred!" Winston cried. "Right again!"

"Poor Hildy," Francie whispered back.

"Winston?" Hildy tugged on his jacket again.

"What is it, Hildy?" Winston asked.

"I don't think anyone wants to do math problems, either."

"No?" Winston said. "Well, I bet they'd love to hear me recite the alphabet backwards." He closed his eyes and began. "Z . . . Y . . . X . . . W . . ."

"Now's our chance," Francie said. "Let's get out of here." She tiptoed toward the door.

"T . . . S . . . R . . ."

"Wait for me!" whispered Otis.

"P . . . O . . . N . . ."

By now a whole stream of guests was tiptoeing out of the room.

"Oh, no." Hildy sank onto the couch and put her head in her hands. The front door opened and closed again and again.

"I . . . H . . . G . . ."

"My party." Hildy moaned. "It's ruined."

"C . . . B . . . A!" Winston cried.

He opened his eyes and looked around the empty room. "My word," he exclaimed. "Where is everyone?"

"Where's Moose?" Hildy groaned. "That's what I want to know."

HAIR
POLISH

Chapter Six

# A Friend in Need

Moose was at home, combing his hair and trimming his whiskers.

He took special care with his bumps. By the time he finished polishing them, he was late.

*Hildy and I still have time for that game of checkers after Winston leaves*, he thought happily, as he hurried up the path.

Hildy's house was strangely quiet. No music, no laughter, nothing.

Moose heard whispers coming from the backyard. Then a few giggles.

Dark shadows danced and pranced around in the dark.

*Hmmm*, Moose thought. *What's going on?*

"Sorry I'm late!" he called as he opened the door. The lights were blazing, but the living room was empty. So was the dining room. Moose found Hildy sitting in the kitchen by herself.

"Where is everyone?" he asked.

"They left." Hildy looked up at him with huge eyes. "Winston kept talking and talking and talking. They couldn't take it anymore."

"Oh, dear." Moose sat down. "I was afraid of this."

Hildy told him what had happened. "By the time he finished with the alphabet," she said, "I was the only one left."

"Oh, my." Moose shook his head. "Where's Winston now?"

"Up in his room." Hildy looked glum. "He said he's not coming out until it's time to catch his train."

"That's not until tomorrow afternoon."

"I know."

“I hate to say it,” Moose said, “but it serves him right.”

“I know it does.” Hildy sighed. “That doesn’t make me feel any better.”

“Me, neither.”

The kitchen felt very empty under the bright lights.

“Everyone left without eating my beautiful cake, too,” said Hildy.

"They didn't go far." Moose stood up. "They're in your backyard, playing night tag. You go tell them it's safe to come in. I'll go talk to Winston."

## Chapter Seven

# Let's Get this Party Hopping

Winston was sitting on his bed. He was slowly putting his clothes into his suitcase, one sock at a time.

"What are you doing?" said Moose.

"Packing."

"Are you okay?"

Winston looked up. "No one even stayed to hear me get to A," he said.

"Maybe they got tired of you showing off," Moose said gently.

"Is that what I do?"

Moose nodded. "Pretty much."

There was a short silence.

"What am I supposed to do?" Winston said.

"You might try listening for a change," Moose said. "You could ask people a few questions about themselves."

Winston looked so sad, Moose took pity on him. "What's that?" he asked. He pointed to a small metal object lying on the bed.

"This?" said Winston. He picked it up. "It's just my old harmonica."

"I didn't know you played the harmonica," said Moose.

"I'm not sure you could call it playing."

"Are you any good?"

"Not really. I play for fun."

"Are you sure you're not an *expert* on harmonicas?" said Moose. "You're absolutely positive?"

A glimmer appeared in Winston's eyes. "You're making fun of me, aren't you, Moose?" he said.

"Not at all," said Moose. "I'm teasing you. That's what friends do."

"Friends?" Winston said, surprised. "Are you and I friends?"

"As long as you promise you won't start

acting like an expert on harmonicas, we are," said Moose. "Come with me and bring that thing with you."

"Where are we going?" Winston cried, jumping up.

"Downstairs." Moose turned to him with a wink. "You and I are going to get this party hopping."

Chapter Eight

# They Like Me!

Winston played his harmonica. Moose grabbed a washboard. Otis ran home and came back with a fiddle. And Francie played the spoons.

The last guest stopped dancing at midnight. Moose, Hildy, and Winston stood at the door waving good night.

There was a chorus of "Come back soon, Winston!" and "Great to meet you, Winston!" as the guests disappeared into the night.

The three hosts fell onto chairs in front of the fire.

"They liked me," Winston said, amazed.

"They really liked me."

"Of course they liked you," said Hildy. "You sounded great."

"Only because Moose drowned me out," Winston said. "Thanks, Moose."

"My pleasure," said Moose.

"You're making fun of me again, aren't you?" Winston laughed.

"Actually, this time I am."

Winston threw a pillow at him. Moose ducked.

"I can't believe you two still have the energy to fool around," Hildy said.

She went into the kitchen and made some hot chocolate. Moose bent down to put another log on the fire.

"What happened to the top of your head?" Winston said. "Did you bump into something?"

"It's my antlers," said Moose. "They're growing back."

Hildy came back with three cups of hot chocolate covered with marshmallows. "They drop off every spring and grow back every fall," she told Winston. "We usually celebrate."

"Oh?" he said. "What do you do?"

Moose and Hildy looked at each other.

"We usually play checkers in front of the fire," Hildy said.

"It's my favorite game," said Moose.

"Great," said Winston. "Can I play?"

"But you said checkers is babyish," Hildy said.

"Does Moose look like a baby to you?" Winston asked with a chuckle. "Besides, friends do things their friends like to do, right?"

"Right."

"Well then," Winston said, "bring out the board!"

8-6-05

## Chapter Nine

# An Expert on Checkers

The next day Moose and Hildy drove Winston to the train station.

"I'm so glad you came, Winston," Hildy said.

"I had a wonderful time," said Winston. "When I don't hog the conversation, I have a lot of fun."

"Hey! I thought you were never funny," Moose said. "You just cracked a joke."

"I did?"

"Hog the conversation?" said Moose. "Hog? You're a pig?"

"Say. . . ." Winston's eyes lit up. "That's pretty funny, isn't it?"

Moose and Hildy laughed.

"I guess if I stop being such a bore, I'll have more fun, right?" Winston slapped his leg. "Bore? *Boar*? Get it?"

"Got it."

Moose parked the car. Winton took his suitcase out of the trunk. They got to the train platform just as the train whistle sounded in the distance.

"I'm going to miss you, Winston," Hildy said, giving him a hug.

"I'll come back," said Winston. "And when I do, you'd better be ready for a rematch, Moose."

"I'll start practicing the minute I get home," Moose promised.

The train pulled into the station. Winston climbed on board and found a seat.

"Good-bye, Winston!" Hildy yelled, as the train started to move. "Come back soon!"

"Don't be a stranger," called Moose.

"I'll get you the next time, Moose!" Winston shouted out the window. "I was rusty!"

The train was gone in a cloud of smoke.

"Winston bought a book titled *Checkers for Advanced Players* this morning," Hildy said, as they walked back to the car. "He's probably going to be an expert by his next visit."

"He'll be a total *bore* about it, too," Moose said. "Good old Winston."